WONDER BOOKS®

Downhill Skiing

A Level Two Reader

By Cynthia Klingel

The Child's World®

It is winter and time to

go skiing!

You must ski on a mountain or very tall hill. Most skiers go to ski resorts.

Skiing takes some special equipment and some practice. It is important to have someone help you get the right equipment when you begin to ski.

First, you need warm clothes. You will want a coat and snow or ski pants. A hat and mittens will protect you from the cold. Wearing a helmet is also a good idea.

Next, you need skis. The skis must be the right length. This depends on how tall you are.

You will need special boots. These boots attach to bindings on the top of the skis. It is important that your boots fit well. Your bindings must be set properly.

Most beginning skiers do not use poles. Poles help more advanced skiers keep their balance, turn, and ski faster.

Now you are ready! You must learn to keep your balance, steer, turn, and stop. A lesson will help you learn.

How do you get to the top? The ski lift brings you to the top of the ski run. Sometimes it is tricky getting on and off.

You did it! Skiing can be so much fun! It is a great winter sport.

Index

To Find Out More

Books

Alba, Gene. *Mutely Goes Skiing.* Torrance, Calif.: Heian, 1998.

Brimmer, Larry Dane. *Skiing.* Danbury, Conn.: Children's Press, 1997.

Dieterich, Michele. *Skiing.* Minneapolis, Minn.: Lerner, 1992.

Simon, Francesca, and Ailie Busby. *Camels Don't Ski.* New York: Sterling Publications, 1998.

Web Sites

Visit our homepage for lots of links about downhill skiing:
http://www.childsworld.com/links.html

Note to Parents, Teachers, and Librarians:
We routinely verify our Web links to make sure they're safe, active sites—so encourage your readers to check them out!

Note to Parents and Educators

Welcome to Wonder Books®! These books provide text at three different levels for beginning readers to practice and strengthen their reading skills. Additionally, the use of nonfiction text provides readers the valuable opportunity to *read to learn*, not just to learn to read.

These leveled readers allow children to choose books at their level of reading confidence and performance. Nonfiction Level One books offer beginning readers simple language, word choice, and sentence structure as well as a word list. Nonfiction Level Two books feature slightly more difficult vocabulary, longer sentences, and longer total text. In the back of each Nonfiction Level Two book are an index and a list of books and Web sites for finding out more information. Nonfiction Level Three books continue to extend word choice and length of text. In the back of each Nonfiction Level Three book are a glossary, an index, and a list of books and Web sites for further research.

State and national standards in reading and language arts emphasize using nonfiction at all levels of reading development. Wonder Books® fill the historical void in nonfiction material for primary grade readers with the additional benefit of a leveled text.

About the Author

Cynthia Klingel has worked as a high school English teacher and an elementary school teacher. She is currently the curriculum director for a Minnesota school district. Cynthia lives with her family in Mankato, Minnesota.

Readers should remember...
All sports carry a certain amount of risk. To reduce the risk of injury while downhill skiing, ski at your own level, wear all safety gear, and use care and common sense. The publisher and author take no responsibility or liability for injuries resulting from downhill skiing.

Published by The Child's World®
P.O. Box 326
Chanhassen, MN 55317-0326
800-599-READ
www.childsworld.com

Photo Credits
© Karl Weatherly/CORBIS: 6, 17
© Marc Muench/CORBIS: 5
© Mike Chew/CORBIS: cover, 2
© Nancy Ney/CORBIS: 10
© Photomundo/GettyImages/Taxi: 14
© Royalty-Free/CORBIS: 9, 21
© Tom Stewart/CORBIS: 18
© William Sallaz/Duomo/CORBIS: 13

Editorial Directions, Inc.: E. Russell Primm and Emily J. Dolbear, Editors;
Alice K. Flanagan, Photo Researcher

The Child's World®: Mary Berendes, Publishing Director

Library of Congress Cataloging-in-Publication Data
Klingel, Cynthia Fitterer.
  Downhill skiing / by Cynthia Klingel.
    p. cm. — (Wonder books, an easy reader)
Summary: A simple introduction to downhill skiing.
Includes bibliographical references and index.
  ISBN 1-56766-456-3 (lib bdg. : alk. paper)
  1. Downhill skiing—Juvenile literature. [1. Skis and skiing.] I. Title. II. Series: Wonder books (Chanhassen, Minn.)
  GV854.315 .K55 2003
  796.93'5—dc21   2002015151